P9-CAY-278

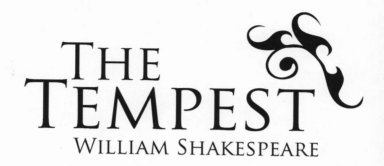

THE
TEMPEST
WILLIAM SHAKESPEARE

CRICKET
HOUSE
BOOKS

At *Cricket House*, it is our desire to create beautiful books.
While the author has already provided the words, we strive to craft an
aesthetic, accessible presentation to showcase their work of art.
From the first page to the last, we want for you, the reader, to not only
immerse yourself in the story, but also own a book that is beautiful
to the eye while in the hand or on the shelf.

We hope you enjoy your read!

This edition copyright © 2010 Cricket House Books, LLC.

PERSONS REPRESENTED

ALONSO, King of Naples

SEBASTIAN, his brother

PROSPERO, the right Duke of Milan

ANTONIO, his brother, the usurping Duke of Milan

FERDINAND, son to the King of Naples

GONZALO, an honest old counsellor

ADRIAN, Lord

FRANCISCO, Lord

CALIBAN, a savage and deformed slave

TRINCULO, a jester

STEPHANO, a drunken butler

MASTER of a ship

BOATSWAIN

MARINERS

MIRANDA, daughter to Prospero

ARIEL, an airy Spirit

IRIS, presented by Spirits

CERES, presented by Spirits

JUNO, presented by Spirits

NYMPHS, presented by Spirits

REAPERS, presented by Spirits

Other Spirits attending on Prospero

SCENE: The sea, with a ship; afterwards an island

ACT I

Scene 1.

[On a ship at sea; a tempestuous noise of thunder and lightning heard]

[Enter a Shipmaster and a Boatswain severally]

MASTER
Boatswain!

BOATSWAIN
Here, master: what cheer?

MASTER
Good! Speak to the mariners: fall to't yarely, or we run ourselves aground: bestir, bestir.

[Exit]

[Enter Mariners]

BOATSWAIN
Heigh, my hearts! cheerly, cheerly, my hearts! yare, yare! Take in the topsail. Tend to th' master's whistle.—Blow till thou burst thy wind, if room enough.

[Enter Alonso, Sebastian, Antonio, Ferdinand, Gonzalo, and Others]

ALONSO
Good boatswain, have care. Where's the master?
Play the men.

BOATSWAIN
I pray now, keep below.

ANTONIO
Where is the master, boson?

BOATSWAIN
Do you not hear him? You mar our labour: keep your cabins:
you do assist the storm.

GONZALO
Nay, good, be patient.

BOATSWAIN
When the sea is. Hence! What cares these roarers for the name of
king? To cabin! silence! Trouble us not.

GONZALO
Good, yet remember whom thou hast aboard.

BOATSWAIN
None that I more love than myself. You are counsellor: if you can
command these elements to silence, and work the peace of the
present, we will not hand a rope more. Use your authority: if you
cannot, give thanks you have lived so long, and make yourself
ready in your cabin for the mischance of the hour, if it so hap.—
Cheerly, good hearts!—Out of our way, I say.

[Exit]

GONZALO
I have great comfort from this fellow. Methinks he hath no drowning mark upon him: his complexion is perfect gallows. Stand fast,
good Fate, to his hanging! make the rope of his destiny our cable,
for our own doth little advantage! If he be not born to be hang'd,
our case is miserable.

[Exeunt]

[Re-enter Boatswain]

BOATSWAIN
Down with the topmast! yare! lower, lower! Bring her to try wi' th' maincourse. *[A cry within]* A plague upon this howling! They are louder than the weather or our office.—

[Re-enter Sebastian, Antonio, and Gonzalo]

Yet again! What do you here? Shall we give o'er, and drown? Have you a mind to sink?

SEBASTIAN
A pox o' your throat, you bawling, blasphemous, incharitable dog!

BOATSWAIN
Work you, then.

ANTONIO
Hang, cur, hang! you whoreson, insolent noisemaker, we are less afraid to be drowned than thou art.

GONZALO
I'll warrant him for drowning, though the ship were no stronger than a nutshell, and as leaky as an unstanched wench.

BOATSWAIN
Lay her a-hold, a-hold! set her two courses: off to sea again: lay her off.

[Enter Mariners, wet]

MARINERS
All lost! to prayers, to prayers! all lost!

[Exeunt]

BOATSWAIN
What, must our mouths be cold?

GONZALO
The King and Prince at prayers! let us assist them,
For our case is as theirs.

SEBASTIAN
I am out of patience.

ANTONIO
We are merely cheated of our lives by drunkards.—
This wide-chapp'd rascal—would thou might'st lie drowning
The washing of ten tides!

GONZALO
He'll be hang'd yet,
Though every drop of water swear against it,
And gape at wid'st to glut him.

[A confused noise within:—'Mercy on us!'—
'We split, we split!'—'Farewell, my wife and children!'—
'Farewell, brother!'—'We split, we split, we split!'—]

ANTONIO
Let's all sink wi' the King.

[Exit]

SEBASTIAN
Let's take leave of him.

[Exit]

GONZALO

Now would I give a thousand furlongs of sea for an acre of barren ground; long heath, brown furze, any thing. The wills above be done! but I would fain die dry death.

[Exit]

Scene II.

[The Island. Before the cell of Prospero.]

[Enter Prospero and Miranda]

MIRANDA

If by your art, my dearest father, you have
Put the wild waters in this roar, allay them.
The sky, it seems, would pour down stinking pitch,
But that the sea, mounting to th' welkin's cheek,
Dashes the fire out. O! I have suffered
With those that I saw suffer: a brave vessel,
Who had, no doubt, some noble creatures in her,
Dash'd all to pieces. O! the cry did knock
Against my very heart. Poor souls, they perish'd.
Had I been any god of power, I would
Have sunk the sea within the earth, or e'er
It should the good ship so have swallow'd and
The fraughting souls within her.

PROSPERO

Be collected:
No more amazement: tell your piteous heart
There's no harm done.

MIRANDA

O! woe the day!

PROSPERO
No harm.
I have done nothing but in care of thee,
Of thee, my dear one, thee, my daughter, who
Art ignorant of what thou art, nought knowing
Of whence I am: nor that I am more better
Than Prospero, master of a full poor cell,
And thy no greater father.

MIRANDA
More to know
Did never meddle with my thoughts.

PROSPERO
'Tis time
I should inform thee farther. Lend thy hand,
And pluck my magic garment from me.—So:

[Lays down his mantle]

Lie there my art.—Wipe thou thine eyes; have comfort.
The direful spectacle of the wrack, which touch'd
The very virtue of compassion in thee,
I have with such provision in mine art
So safely ordered that there is no soul—
No, not so much perdition as an hair
Betid to any creature in the vessel
Which thou heard'st cry, which thou saw'st sink. Sit down;
For thou must now know farther.

MIRANDA
You have often
Begun to tell me what I am: but stopp'd,
And left me to a bootless inquisition,
Concluding 'Stay; not yet.'

PROSPERO
The hour's now come,
The very minute bids thee ope thine ear;
Obey, and be attentive. Canst thou remember
A time before we came unto this cell?
I do not think thou canst: for then thou wast not
Out three years old.

MIRANDA
Certainly, sir, I can.

PROSPERO
By what? By any other house, or person?
Of any thing the image, tell me, that
Hath kept with thy remembrance.

MIRANDA
'Tis far off,
And rather like a dream than an assurance
That my remembrance warrants. Had I not
Four, or five, women once, that tended me?

PROSPERO
Thou hadst, and more, Miranda. But how is it
That this lives in thy mind? What seest thou else
In the dark backward and abysm of time?
If thou rememb'rest aught ere thou cam'st here,
How thou cam'st here, thou mayst.

MIRANDA
But that I do not.

PROSPERO
Twelve year since, Miranda, twelve year since,
Thy father was the Duke of Milan, and
A prince of power.

MIRANDA
Sir, are not you my father?

PROSPERO
Thy mother was a piece of virtue, and
She said thou wast my daughter: and thy father
Was Duke of Milan, and his only heir
And princess,—no worse issued.

MIRANDA
O, the heavens!
What foul play had we that we came from thence?
Or blessed was't we did?

PROSPERO
Both, both, my girl.
By foul play, as thou say'st, were we heav'd thence;
But blessedly holp hither.

MIRANDA
O! my heart bleeds
To think o' th' teen that I have turn'd you to,
Which is from my remembrance. Please you, further.

PROSPERO
My brother and thy uncle, call'd Antonio—
I pray thee, mark me,—that a brother should
Be so perfidious!—he, whom next thyself,
Of all the world I lov'd, and to him put
The manage of my state; as at that time
Through all the signories it was the first,
And Prospero the prime duke, being so reputed
In dignity, and for the liberal arts,
Without a parallel: those being all my study,
The government I cast upon my brother,
And to my state grew stranger, being transported

And rapt in secret studies. Thy false uncle—
Dost thou attend me?

MIRANDA
Sir, most heedfully.

PROSPERO
Being once perfected how to grant suits,
How to deny them, who t' advance, and who
To trash for over-topping; new created
The creatures that were mine, I say, or chang'd 'em,
Or else new form'd 'em: having both the key
Of officer and office, set all hearts i' th' state
To what tune pleas'd his ear: that now he was
The ivy which had hid my princely trunk,
And suck'd my verdure out on't.—Thou attend'st not.

MIRANDA
O, good sir! I do.

PROSPERO
I pray thee, mark me.
I thus neglecting worldly ends, all dedicated
To closeness and the bettering of my mind
With that, which, but by being so retir'd,
O'er-priz'd all popular rate, in my false brother
Awak'd an evil nature; and my trust,
Like a good parent, did beget of him
A falsehood, in its contrary as great
As my trust was; which had indeed no limit,
A confidence sans bound. He being thus lorded,
Not only with what my revenue yielded,
But what my power might else exact,—like one
Who having, into truth, by telling of it,
Made such a sinner of his memory,
To credit his own lie,—he did believe

He was indeed the Duke; out o' the substitution,
And executing th' outward face of royalty,
With all prerogative.—Hence his ambition growing—
Dost thou hear?

MIRANDA
Your tale, sir, would cure deafness.

PROSPERO
To have no screen between this part he play'd
And him he play'd it for, he needs will be
Absolute Milan. Me, poor man—my library
Was dukedom large enough: of temporal royalties
He thinks me now incapable; confederates,—
So dry he was for sway,—wi' th' King of Naples
To give him annual tribute, do him homage;
Subject his coronet to his crown, and bend
The dukedom, yet unbow'd—alas, poor Milan!—
To most ignoble stooping.

MIRANDA
O the heavens!

PROSPERO
Mark his condition, and the event; then tell me
If this might be a brother.

MIRANDA
I should sin
To think but nobly of my grandmother:
Good wombs have borne bad sons.

PROSPERO
Now the condition.
This King of Naples, being an enemy
To me inveterate, hearkens my brother's suit;

Which was, that he, in lieu o' the premises
Of homage and I know not how much tribute,
Should presently extirpate me and mine
Out of the dukedom, and confer fair Milan,
With all the honours on my brother: whereon,
A treacherous army levied, one midnight
Fated to the purpose, did Antonio open
The gates of Milan; and, i' th' dead of darkness,
The ministers for th' purpose hurried thence
Me and thy crying self.

MIRANDA
Alack, for pity!
I, not rememb'ring how I cried out then,
Will cry it o'er again: it is a hint
That wrings mine eyes to't.

PROSPERO
Hear a little further,
And then I'll bring thee to the present business
Which now's upon us; without the which this story
Were most impertinent.

MIRANDA
Wherefore did they not
That hour destroy us?

PROSPERO
Well demanded, wench:
My tale provokes that question. Dear, they durst not,
So dear the love my people bore me, nor set
A mark so bloody on the business; but
With colours fairer painted their foul ends.
In few, they hurried us aboard a bark,
Bore us some leagues to sea, where they prepared
A rotten carcass of a boat, not rigg'd,

Nor tackle, sail, nor mast: the very rats
Instinctively have quit it. There they hoist us,
To cry to th' sea, that roar'd to us: to sigh
To th' winds, whose pity, sighing back again,
Did us but loving wrong.

MIRANDA
Alack! what trouble
Was I then to you!

PROSPERO
O, a cherubin
Thou wast that did preserve me! Thou didst smile,
Infused with a fortitude from heaven,
When I have deck'd the sea with drops full salt,
Under my burden groan'd: which rais'd in me
An undergoing stomach, to bear up
Against what should ensue.

MIRANDA
How came we ashore?

PROSPERO
By Providence divine.
Some food we had and some fresh water that
A noble Neapolitan, Gonzalo,
Out of his charity,—who being then appointed
Master of this design,—did give us, with
Rich garments, linens, stuffs, and necessaries,
Which since have steaded much: so, of his gentleness,
Knowing I lov'd my books, he furnish'd me,
From mine own library with volumes that
I prize above my dukedom.

MIRANDA
Would I might
But ever see that man!

PROSPERO
Now I arise:—

[Resumes his mantle]

Sit still, and hear the last of our sea-sorrow.
Here in this island we arriv'd: and here
Have I, thy schoolmaster, made thee more profit
Than other princes can, that have more time
For vainer hours, and tutors not so careful.

MIRANDA
Heavens thank you for't! And now, I pray you, sir,—
For still 'tis beating in my mind,—your reason
For raising this sea-storm?

PROSPERO
Know thus far forth.
By accident most strange, bountiful Fortune,
Now my dear lady, hath mine enemies
Brought to this shore; and by my prescience
I find my zenith doth depend upon
A most auspicious star, whose influence
If now I court not but omit, my fortunes
Will ever after droop. Here cease more questions;
Thou art inclin'd to sleep; 'tis a good dulness,
And give it way;—I know thou canst not choose.—

[Miranda sleeps]

Come away, servant, come! I am ready now.
Approach, my Ariel; Come!

[Enter Ariel]

ARIEL
All hail, great master! grave sir, hail! I come
To answer thy best pleasure; be't to fly,
To swim, to dive into the fire, to ride
On the curl'd clouds; to thy strong bidding task
Ariel and all his quality.

PROSPERO
Hast thou, spirit,
Perform'd to point the tempest that I bade thee?

ARIEL
To every article.
I boarded the King's ship; now on the beak,
Now in the waist, the deck, in every cabin,
I flam'd amazement; sometime I'd divide,
And burn in many places; on the topmast,
The yards, and boresprit, would I flame distinctly,
Then meet and join: Jove's lightning, the precursors
O' th' dreadful thunder-claps, more momentary
And sight-outrunning were not: the fire and cracks
Of sulphurous roaring the most mighty Neptune
Seem to besiege and make his bold waves tremble,
Yea, his dread trident shake.

PROSPERO
My brave spirit!
Who was so firm, so constant, that this coil
Would not infect his reason?

ARIEL
Not a soul
But felt a fever of the mad, and play'd
Some tricks of desperation. All but mariners
Plunged in the foaming brine and quit the vessel,
Then all afire with me: the King's son, Ferdinand,

With hair up-staring—then like reeds, not hair—
Was the first man that leapt; cried 'Hell is empty,
And all the devils are here.'

PROSPERO
Why, that's my spirit!
But was not this nigh shore?

ARIEL
Close by, my master.

PROSPERO
But are they, Ariel, safe?

ARIEL
Not a hair perish'd;
On their sustaining garments not a blemish,
But fresher than before: and, as thou bad'st me,
In troops I have dispers'd them 'bout the isle.
The king's son have I landed by himself,
Whom I left cooling of the air with sighs
In an odd angle of the isle, and sitting,
His arms in this sad knot.

PROSPERO
Of the King's ship
The mariners, say how thou hast dispos'd,
And all the rest o' th' fleet?

ARIEL
Safely in harbour
Is the King's ship; in the deep nook, where once
Thou call'dst me up at midnight to fetch dew
From the still-vex'd Bermoothes; there she's hid:
The mariners all under hatches stowed;
Who, with a charm join'd to their suff'red labour,

I have left asleep: and for the rest o' th' fleet
Which I dispers'd, they all have met again,
And are upon the Mediterranean flote
Bound sadly home for Naples,
Supposing that they saw the king's ship wrack'd,
And his great person perish.

PROSPERO
Ariel, thy charge
Exactly is perform'd; but there's more work:
What is the time o' th' day?

ARIEL
Past the mid season.

PROSPERO
At least two glasses. The time 'twixt six and now
Must by us both be spent most preciously.

ARIEL
Is there more toil? Since thou dost give me pains,
Let me remember thee what thou hast promis'd,
Which is not yet perform'd me.

PROSPERO
How now! moody?
What is't thou canst demand?

ARIEL
My liberty.

PROSPERO
Before the time be out! No more!

ARIEL
I prithee,
Remember I have done thee worthy service;

Told thee no lies, made no mistakings, serv'd
Without or grudge or grumblings: thou didst promise
To bate me a full year.

PROSPERO
Dost thou forget
From what a torment I did free thee?

ARIEL
No.

PROSPERO
Thou dost; and think'st it much to tread the ooze
Of the salt deep,
To run upon the sharp wind of the north,
To do me business in the veins o' th' earth
When it is bak'd with frost.

ARIEL
I do not, sir.

PROSPERO
Thou liest, malignant thing! Hast thou forgot
The foul witch Sycorax, who with age and envy
Was grown into a hoop? Hast thou forgot her?

ARIEL
No, sir.

PROSPERO
Thou hast. Where was she born?
Speak; tell me.

ARIEL
Sir, in Argier.

PROSPERO
O! was she so? I must
Once in a month recount what thou hast been,
Which thou forget'st. This damn'd witch Sycorax,
For mischiefs manifold, and sorceries terrible
To enter human hearing, from Argier,
Thou know'st,was banish'd: for one thing she did
They would not take her life. Is not this true?

ARIEL
Ay, sir.

PROSPERO
This blue-ey'd hag was hither brought with child,
And here was left by the sailors. Thou, my slave,
As thou report'st thyself, wast then her servant:
And, for thou wast a spirit too delicate
To act her earthy and abhorr'd commands,
Refusing her grand hests, she did confine thee,
By help of her more potent ministers,
And in her most unmitigable rage,
Into a cloven pine; within which rift
Imprison'd, thou didst painfully remain
A dozen years; within which space she died,
And left thee there, where thou didst vent thy groans
As fast as mill-wheels strike. Then was this island—
Save for the son that she did litter here,
A freckl'd whelp, hag-born—not honour'd with
A human shape.

ARIEL
Yes; Caliban her son.

PROSPERO
Dull thing, I say so; he, that Caliban,
Whom now I keep in service. Thou best know'st

What torment I did find thee in; thy groans
Did make wolves howl, and penetrate the breasts
Of ever-angry bears: it was a torment
To lay upon the damn'd, which Sycorax
Could not again undo; it was mine art,
When I arriv'd and heard thee, that made gape
The pine, and let thee out.

ARIEL
I thank thee, master.

PROSPERO
If thou more murmur'st, I will rend an oak
And peg thee in his knotty entrails till
Thou hast howl'd away twelve winters.

ARIEL
Pardon, master:
I will be correspondent to command,
And do my spriting gently.

PROSPERO
Do so; and after two days
I will discharge thee.

ARIEL
That's my noble master!
What shall I do? Say what? What shall I do?

PROSPERO
Go make thyself like a nymph o' th' sea: be subject
To no sight but thine and mine; invisible
To every eyeball else. Go, take this shape,
And hither come in 't: go, hence with diligence!

[Exit Ariel]

Awake, dear heart, awake! thou hast slept well;
Awake!

MIRANDA
[Waking] The strangeness of your story put
Heaviness in me.

PROSPERO
Shake it off. Come on;
We'll visit Caliban my slave, who never
Yields us kind answer.

MIRANDA
'Tis a villain, sir,
I do not love to look on.

PROSPERO
But as 'tis,
We cannot miss him: he does make our fire,
Fetch in our wood; and serves in offices
That profit us.—What ho! slave! Caliban!
Thou earth, thou! Speak.

CALIBAN
[Within] There's wood enough within.

PROSPERO
Come forth, I say; there's other business for thee:
Come, thou tortoise! when?

[Re-enter Ariel like a water-nymph.]

Fine apparition! My quaint Ariel,
Hark in thine ear.

ARIEL
My lord, it shall be done.

[Exit]

PROSPERO
Thou poisonous slave, got by the devil himself
Upon thy wicked dam, come forth!

[Enter Caliban]

CALIBAN
As wicked dew as e'er my mother brush'd
With raven's feather from unwholesome fen
Drop on you both! A south-west blow on ye,
And blister you all o'er!

PROSPERO
For this, be sure, to-night thou shalt have cramps,
Side-stitches that shall pen thy breath up; urchins
Shall forth at vast of night that they may work
All exercise on thee: thou shalt be pinch'd
As thick as honeycomb, each pinch more stinging
Than bees that made them.

CALIBAN
I must eat my dinner.
This island's mine, by Sycorax my mother,
Which thou tak'st from me. When thou cam'st first,
Thou strok'st me and made much of me; wouldst give me
Water with berries in't; and teach me how
To name the bigger light, and how the less,
That burn by day and night: and then I lov'd thee,
And show'd thee all the qualities o' th' isle,
The fresh springs, brine-pits, barren place, and fertile.
Curs'd be I that did so! All the charms
Of Sycorax, toads, beetles, bats, light on you!
For I am all the subjects that you have,
Which first was mine own king; and here you sty me

In this hard rock, whiles you do keep from me
The rest o' th' island.

PROSPERO
Thou most lying slave,
Whom stripes may move, not kindness! I have us'd thee,
Filth as thou art, with human care, and lodg'd thee
In mine own cell, till thou didst seek to violate
The honour of my child.

CALIBAN
Oh ho! Oh ho! Would it had been done!
Thou didst prevent me; I had peopl'd else
This isle with Calibans.

PROSPERO
Abhorred slave,
Which any print of goodness wilt not take,
Being capable of all ill! I pitied thee,
Took pains to make thee speak, taught thee each hour
One thing or other: when thou didst not, savage,
Know thine own meaning, but wouldst gabble like
A thing most brutish, I endow'd thy purposes
With words that made them known: but thy vile race,
Though thou didst learn, had that in't which good natures
Could not abide to be with; therefore wast thou
Deservedly confin'd into this rock, who hadst
Deserv'd more than a prison.

CALIBAN
You taught me language, and my profit on't
Is, I know how to curse: the red plague rid you,
For learning me your language!

PROSPERO
Hag-seed, hence!
Fetch us in fuel; and be quick, thou 'rt best,

To answer other business. Shrug'st thou, malice?
If thou neglect'st, or dost unwillingly
What I command, I'll rack thee with old cramps,
Fill all thy bones with aches; make thee roar,
That beasts shall tremble at thy din.

CALIBAN
No, pray thee.—
[Aside] I must obey. His art is of such power,
It would control my dam's god, Setebos,
And make a vassal of him.

PROSPERO
So, slave: hence!

[Exit Caliban]

[Re-enter Ariel invisible, playing and singing; Ferdinand following]

[Ariel's Song.]
Come unto these yellow sands,
And then take hands:
Curtsied when you have, and kiss'd,—
The wild waves whist,—
Foot it featly here and there;
And, sweet sprites, the burden bear.
Hark, hark!
    [Burden: Bow, wow, dispersedly.]
The watch dogs bark:
    [Burden: Bow, wow, dispersedly.]
Hark, hark! I hear
The strain of strutting Chanticleer
    [Cry, Cock-a-diddle-dow.]

FERDINAND
Where should this music be? i' th' air or th' earth?
It sounds no more;—and sure it waits upon

Some god o' th' island. Sitting on a bank,
Weeping again the king my father's wrack,
This music crept by me upon the waters,
Allaying both their fury and my passion,
With its sweet air: thence I have follow'd it,—
Or it hath drawn me rather,—but 'tis gone.
No, it begins again.

[Ariel sings]
Full fathom five thy father lies:
Of his bones are coral made:
Those are pearls that were his eyes:
Nothing of him that doth fade
But doth suffer a sea-change
Into something rich and strange.
Sea-nymphs hourly ring his knell:
  [Burden: Ding-dong.]
Hark! now I hear them—ding-dong, bell.

FERDINAND
The ditty does remember my drown'd father.
This is no mortal business, nor no sound
That the earth owes:—I hear it now above me.

PROSPERO
The fringed curtains of thine eye advance,
And say what thou seest yond.

MIRANDA
What is't? a spirit?
Lord, how it looks about! Believe me, sir,
It carries a brave form:—but 'tis a spirit.

PROSPERO
No, wench; it eats and sleeps, and hath such senses
As we have, such; this gallant which thou see'st

Was in the wrack; and but he's something stain'd
With grief,—that beauty's canker,—thou mightst call him
A goodly person: he hath lost his fellows
And strays about to find 'em.

MIRANDA
I might call him
A thing divine; for nothing natural
I ever saw so noble.

PROSPERO
[Aside] It goes on, I see,
As my soul prompts it.—Spirit, fine spirit! I'll free thee
Within two days for this.

FERDINAND
Most sure, the goddess
On whom these airs attend!—Vouchsafe, my prayer
May know if you remain upon this island;
And that you will some good instruction give
How I may bear me here: my prime request,
Which I do last pronounce, is,—O you wonder!—
If you be maid or no?

MIRANDA
No wonder, sir;
But certainly a maid.

FERDINAND
My language! Heavens!—
I am the best of them that speak this speech,
Were I but where 'tis spoken.

PROSPERO
How! the best?
What wert thou, if the King of Naples heard thee?

FERDINAND
A single thing, as I am now, that wonders
To hear thee speak of Naples. He does hear me;
And, that he does, I weep: myself am Naples,
Who with mine eyes,—never since at ebb,—beheld
The King, my father wrack'd.

MIRANDA
Alack, for mercy!

FERDINAND
Yes, faith, and all his lords, the Duke of Milan,
And his brave son being twain.

PROSPERO
[Aside.] The Duke of Milan,
And his more braver daughter could control thee,
If now 'twere fit to do't.—At the first sight *[Aside.]*
They have changed eyes;—delicate Ariel,
I'll set thee free for this!—*[To Ferdinand]* A word, good sir:
I fear you have done yourself some wrong: a word.

MIRANDA
[Aside.] Why speaks my father so ungently? This
Is the third man that e'er I saw; the first
That e'er I sigh'd for; pity move my father
To be inclin'd my way!

FERDINAND
[Aside.] O! if a virgin,
And your affection not gone forth, I'll make you
The Queen of Naples.

PROSPERO
Soft, sir; one word more—
[Aside] They are both in either's powers: but this swift

business I must uneasy make, lest too light winning
Make the prize light. *[To Ferdinand]* One word more:
    I charge thee
That thou attend me. Thou dost here usurp
The name thou ow'st not; and hast put thyself
Upon this island as a spy, to win it
From me, the lord on't.

FERDINAND
No, as I am a man.

MIRANDA
There's nothing ill can dwell in such a temple:
If the ill spirit have so fair a house,
Good things will strive to dwell with't.

PROSPERO
[To Ferdinand] Follow me.—
[To Miranda] Speak not you for him; he's a traitor.—
[To Ferdinand] Come;
I'll manacle thy neck and feet together:
Sea-water shalt thou drink; thy food shall be
The fresh-brook mussels, wither'd roots, and husks
Wherein the acorn cradled. Follow.

FERDINAND
No;
I will resist such entertainment till
Mine enemy has more power.

[He draws, and is charmed from moving.]

MIRANDA
O dear father!
Make not too rash a trial of him, for
He's gentle, and not fearful.

PROSPERO
What! I say,
My foot my tutor? Put thy sword up, traitor;
Who mak'st a show, but dar'st not strike, thy conscience
Is so possess'd with guilt: come from thy ward,
For I can here disarm thee with this stick
And make thy weapon drop.

MIRANDA
Beseech you, father!

PROSPERO
Hence! Hang not on my garments.

MIRANDA
Sir, have pity;
I'll be his surety.

PROSPERO
Silence! One word more
Shall make me chide thee, if not hate thee. What!
An advocate for an impostor? hush!
Thou think'st there is no more such shapes as he,
Having seen but him and Caliban: foolish wench!
To the most of men this is a Caliban,
And they to him are angels.

MIRANDA
My affections
Are then most humble; I have no ambition
To see a goodlier man.

PROSPERO
[To Ferdinand] Come on; obey:
Thy nerves are in their infancy again,
And have no vigour in them.

FERDINAND
So they are:
My spirits, as in a dream, are all bound up.
My father's loss, the weakness which I feel,
The wrack of all my friends, nor this man's threats,
To whom I am subdued, are but light to me,
Might I but through my prison once a day
Behold this maid: all corners else o' th' earth
Let liberty make use of; space enough
Have I in such a prison.

PROSPERO
[Aside] It works.—*[To Ferdinand]* Come on.—
Thou hast done well, fine Ariel! *[To Ferdinand]* Follow me.—
[To Ariel] Hark what thou else shalt do me.

MIRANDA
Be of comfort;
My father's of a better nature, sir,
Than he appears by speech: this is unwonted,
Which now came from him.

PROSPERO
Thou shalt be as free
As mountain winds; but then exactly do
All points of my command.

ARIEL
To the syllable.

PROSPERO
[To Ferdinand] Come, follow.—Speak not for him.

[Exeunt]

ACT II

Scene 1. Another part of the island

[Enter Alonso, Sebastian, Antonio, Gonzalo, Adrian, Francisco, and Others]

GONZALO
Beseech you, sir, be merry: you have cause,
So have we all, of joy; for our escape
Is much beyond our loss. Our hint of woe
Is common: every day, some sailor's wife,
The masters of some merchant and the merchant,
Have just our theme of woe; but for the miracle,
I mean our preservation, few in millions
Can speak like us: then wisely, good sir, weigh
Our sorrow with our comfort.

ALONSO
Prithee, peace.

SEBASTIAN
He receives comfort like cold porridge.

ANTONIO
The visitor will not give him o'er so.

SEBASTIAN Look, he's winding up the watch of his wit; by and by it will strike.

GONZALO
Sir,—

SEBASTIAN
One: tell.

GONZALO
When every grief is entertain'd that's offer'd,
Comes to the entertainer—

SEBASTIAN
A dollar.

GONZALO
Dolour comes to him, indeed: you have spoken truer than you
purposed.

SEBASTIAN
You have taken it wiselier than I meant you should.

GONZALO
Therefore, my lord,—

ANTONIO
Fie, what a spendthrift is he of his tongue!

ALONSO.
I prithee, spare.

GONZALO
Well, I have done: but yet—

SEBASTIAN
He will be talking.

ANTONIO
Which, of he or Adrian, for a good wager, first begins to crow?

SEBASTIAN
The old cock.

ANTONIO
The cockerel.

SEBASTIAN
Done. The wager?

ANTONIO
A laughter.

SEBASTIAN
A match!

ADRIAN
Though this island seem to be desert,—

SEBASTIAN
Ha, ha, ha! So, you're paid.

ADRIAN
Uninhabitable, and almost inaccessible,—

SEBASTIAN
Yet—

ADRIAN
Yet—

ANTONIO
He could not miss it.

ADRIAN
It must needs be of subtle, tender, and delicate temperance.

ANTONIO
Temperance was a delicate wench.

SEBASTIAN
Ay, and a subtle; as he most learnedly delivered.

ADRIAN
The air breathes upon us here most sweetly.

SEBASTIAN
As if it had lungs, and rotten ones.

ANTONIO
Or, as 'twere perfum'd by a fen.

GONZALO
Here is everything advantageous to life.

ANTONIO
True; save means to live.

SEBASTIAN
Of that there's none, or little.

GONZALO
How lush and lusty the grass looks! how green!

ANTONIO
The ground indeed is tawny.

SEBASTIAN
With an eye of green in't.

ANTONIO
He misses not much.

SEBASTIAN
No; he doth but mistake the truth totally.

GONZALO
But the rarity of it is,—which is indeed almost beyond credit,—

SEBASTIAN
As many vouch'd rarities are.

GONZALO
That our garments, being, as they were, drenched in the sea, hold notwithstanding their freshness and glosses, being rather new-dyed than stain'd with salt water.

ANTONIO
If but one of his pockets could speak, would it not say he lies?

SEBASTIAN
Ay, or very falsely pocket up his report.

GONZALO
Methinks, our garments are now as fresh as when we put them on first in Afric, at the marriage of the king's fair daughter Claribel to the King of Tunis.

SEBASTIAN
'Twas a sweet marriage, and we prosper well in our return.

ADRIAN
Tunis was never graced before with such a paragon to their queen.

GONZALO
Not since widow Dido's time.

ANTONIO
Widow! a pox o' that! How came that widow in? Widow Dido!

SEBASTIAN
What if he had said, widower Aeneas too?
Good Lord, how you take it!

ADRIAN
Widow Dido said you? You make me study of that; she was of Carthage, not of Tunis.

GONZALO
This Tunis, sir, was Carthage.

ADRIAN
Carthage?

GONZALO
I assure you, Carthage.

ANTONIO
His word is more than the miraculous harp.

SEBASTIAN
He hath rais'd the wall, and houses too.

ANTONIO
What impossible matter will he make easy next?

SEBASTIAN
I think he will carry this island home in his pocket, and give it his
son for an apple.

ANTONIO
And, sowing the kernels of it in the sea, bring forth more islands.

ALONSO
Ay.

ANTONIO
Why, in good time.

GONZALO
[To Alonso] Sir, we were talking that our garments seem now as
fresh as when we were at Tunis at the marriage of your daughter,
who is now Queen.

ANTONIO
And the rarest that e'er came there.

SEBASTIAN
Bate, I beseech you, widow Dido.

ANTONIO
O! widow Dido; ay, widow Dido.

GONZALO
Is not, sir, my doublet as fresh as the first day I wore it? I mean, in a sort.

ANTONIO
That sort was well fish'd for.

GONZALO
When I wore it at your daughter's marriage?

ALONSO
You cram these words into mine ears against
The stomach of my sense. Would I had never
Married my daughter there! for, coming thence,
My son is lost; and, in my rate, she too,
Who is so far from Italy remov'd,
I ne'er again shall see her. O thou, mine heir
Of Naples and of Milan! what strange fish
Hath made his meal on thee?

FRANCISCO
Sir, he may live:
I saw him beat the surges under him,
And ride upon their backs: he trod the water,
Whose enmity he flung aside, and breasted
The surge most swoln that met him: his bold head
'Bove the contentious waves he kept, and oar'd

Himself with his good arms in lusty stroke
To th' shore, that o'er his wave-worn basis bowed,
As stooping to relieve him. I not doubt
He came alive to land.

ALONSO
No, no; he's gone.

SEBASTIAN
Sir, you may thank yourself for this great loss,
That would not bless our Europe with your daughter,
But rather lose her to an African;
Where she, at least, is banish'd from your eye,
Who hath cause to wet the grief on't.

ALONSO
Prithee, peace.

SEBASTIAN
You were kneel'd to, and importun'd otherwise
By all of us; and the fair soul herself
Weigh'd between loathness and obedience at
Which end o' th' beam should bow. We have lost your son,
I fear, for ever: Milan and Naples have
More widows in them of this business' making,
Than we bring men to comfort them; the fault's your own.

ALONSO
So is the dearest of the loss.

GONZALO
My lord Sebastian,
The truth you speak doth lack some gentleness
And time to speak it in; you rub the sore,
When you should bring the plaster.

SEBASTIAN
Very well.

ANTONIO
And most chirurgeonly.

GONZALO
It is foul weather in us all, good sir,
When you are cloudy.

SEBASTIAN
Foul weather?

ANTONIO
Very foul.

GONZALO
Had I plantation of this isle, my lord,—

ANTONIO
He'd sow 't with nettle-seed.

SEBASTIAN
Or docks, or mallows.

GONZALO
And were the king on't, what would I do?

SEBASTIAN
'Scape being drunk for want of wine.

GONZALO
I' the commonwealth I would by contraries
Execute all things; for no kind of traffic
Would I admit; no name of magistrate;
Letters should not be known; riches, poverty,

And use of service, none; contract, succession,
Bourn, bound of land, tilth, vineyard, none;
No use of metal, corn, or wine, or oil;
No occupation; all men idle, all:
And women too, but innocent and pure;
No sovereignty,—

SEBASTIAN
Yet he would be king on't.

ANTONIO
The latter end of his commonwealth forgets the beginning.

GONZALO
All things in common nature should produce
Without sweat or endeavour; treason, felony,
Sword, pike, knife, gun, or need of any engine,
Would I not have; but nature should bring forth,
Of it own kind, all foison, all abundance,
To feed my innocent people.

SEBASTIAN
No marrying 'mong his subjects?

ANTONIO
None, man: all idle; whores and knaves.

GONZALO
I would with such perfection govern, sir,
To excel the golden age.

SEBASTIAN
Save his Majesty!

ANTONIO
Long live Gonzalo!

GONZALO
And,—do you mark me, sir?

ALONSO
Prithee, no more: thou dost talk nothing to me.

GONZALO
I do well believe your highness; and did it to minister occasion to
these gentlemen, who are of such sensible and nimble lungs that
they always use to laugh at nothing.

ANTONIO
'Twas you we laugh'd at.

GONZALO
Who in this kind of merry fooling am nothing to you; so you may
continue, and laugh at nothing still.

ANTONIO
What a blow was there given!

SEBASTIAN
An it had not fallen flat-long.

GONZALO
You are gentlemen of brave mettle: you would lift the moon
out of her sphere, if she would continue in it five weeks without
changing.

[Enter Ariel, invisible, playing solemn music]

SEBASTIAN
We would so, and then go a-bat-fowling.

ANTONIO
Nay, good my lord, be not angry.

GONZALO
No, I warrant you; I will not adventure my discretion so weakly.
Will you laugh me asleep, for I am very heavy?

ANTONIO
Go sleep, and hear us.

[All sleep but Alonso, Sebastian, and Antonio]

ALONSO
What! all so soon asleep! I wish mine eyes
Would, with themselves, shut up my thoughts: I find
They are inclin'd to do so.

SEBASTIAN
Please you, sir,
Do not omit the heavy offer of it:
It seldom visits sorrow; when it doth,
It is a comforter.

ANTONIO
We two, my lord,
Will guard your person while you take your rest,
And watch your safety.

ALONSO
Thank you. Wondrous heavy!

[Alonso sleeps. Exit Ariel]

SEBASTIAN
What a strange drowsiness possesses them!

ANTONIO
It is the quality o' th' climate.

SEBASTIAN
Why doth it not then our eyelids sink?
I find not myself dispos'd to sleep.

ANTONIO
Nor I: my spirits are nimble.
They fell together all, as by consent;
They dropp'd, as by a thunder-stroke. What might,
Worthy Sebastian? O! what might?—No more:—
And yet methinks I see it in thy face,
What thou should'st be: The occasion speaks thee; and
My strong imagination sees a crown
Dropping upon thy head.

SEBASTIAN
What! art thou waking?

ANTONIO
Do you not hear me speak?

SEBASTIAN
I do: and surely
It is a sleepy language, and thou speak'st
Out of thy sleep. What is it thou didst say?
This is a strange repose, to be asleep
With eyes wide open; standing, speaking, moving,
And yet so fast asleep.

ANTONIO
Noble Sebastian,
Thou let'st thy fortune sleep—die rather: wink'st
Whiles thou art waking.

SEBASTIAN
Thou dost snore distinctly:
There's meaning in thy snores.

ANTONIO
I am more serious than my custom; you
Must be so too, if heed me: which to do
Trebles thee o'er.

SEBASTIAN
Well, I am standing water.

ANTONIO
I'll teach you how to flow.

SEBASTIAN
Do so: to ebb,
Hereditary sloth instructs me.

ANTONIO
O!
If you but knew how you the purpose cherish
Whiles thus you mock it! how, in stripping it,
You more invest it! Ebbing men indeed,
Most often, do so near the bottom run
By their own fear or sloth.

SEBASTIAN
Prithee, say on:
The setting of thine eye and cheek proclaim
A matter from thee, and a birth, indeed
Which throes thee much to yield.

ANTONIO
Thus, sir:
Although this lord of weak remembrance, this
Who shall be of as little memory
When he is earth'd, hath here almost persuaded,—
For he's a spirit of persuasion, only
Professes to persuade,—the King his son's alive,

'Tis as impossible that he's undrown'd
As he that sleeps here swims.

SEBASTIAN
I have no hope
That he's undrown'd.

ANTONIO
O! out of that 'no hope'
What great hope have you! No hope that way is
Another way so high a hope, that even
Ambition cannot pierce a wink beyond,
But doubts discovery there. Will you grant with me
That Ferdinand is drown'd?

SEBASTIAN
He's gone.

ANTONIO
Then tell me,
Who's the next heir of Naples?

SEBASTIAN
Claribel.

ANTONIO
She that is Queen of Tunis; she that dwells
Ten leagues beyond man's life; she that from Naples
Can have no note, unless the sun were post—
The Man i' th' Moon's too slow—till newborn chins
Be rough and razorable: she that from whom
We all were sea-swallow'd, though some cast again,
And by that destiny, to perform an act
Whereof what's past is prologue, what to come
In yours and my discharge.

SEBASTIAN
What stuff is this!—How say you?
'Tis true, my brother's daughter's Queen of Tunis;
So is she heir of Naples; 'twixt which regions
There is some space.

ANTONIO
A space whose every cubit
Seems to cry out 'How shall that Claribel
Measure us back to Naples?—Keep in Tunis,
And let Sebastian wake.'—Say this were death
That now hath seiz'd them; why, they were no worse
Than now they are. There be that can rule Naples
As well as he that sleeps; lords that can prate
As amply and unnecessarily
As this Gonzalo: I myself could make
A chough of as deep chat. O, that you bore
The mind that I do! What a sleep were this
For your advancement! Do you understand me?

SEBASTIAN
Methinks I do.

ANTONIO
And how does your content
Tender your own good fortune?

SEBASTIAN
I remember
You did supplant your brother Prospero.

ANTONIO
True.
And look how well my garments sit upon me;
Much feater than before; my brother's servants
Were then my fellows; now they are my men.

SEBASTIAN
But, for your conscience,—

ANTONIO
Ay, sir; where lies that? If 'twere a kibe,
'Twould put me to my slipper: but I feel not
This deity in my bosom: twenty consciences
That stand 'twixt me and Milan, candied be they
And melt ere they molest! Here lies your brother,
No better than the earth he lies upon,
If he were that which now he's like, that's dead:
Whom I, with this obedient steel,—three inches of it,—
Can lay to bed for ever; whiles you, doing thus,
To the perpetual wink for aye might put
This ancient morsel, this Sir Prudence, who
Should not upbraid our course. For all the rest,
They'll take suggestion as a cat laps milk:
They'll tell the clock to any business that
We say befits the hour.

SEBASTIAN
Thy case, dear friend,
Shall be my precedent: as thou got'st Milan,
I'll come by Naples. Draw thy sword: one stroke
Shall free thee from the tribute which thou pay'st,
And I the king shall love thee.

ANTONIO
Draw together:
And when I rear my hand, do you the like,
To fall it on Gonzalo.

SEBASTIAN
O! but one word.

[They converse apart.]

[Music. Re-enter Ariel, invisible.]

ARIEL
My master through his art foresees the danger
That you, his friend, are in; and sends me forth—
For else his project dies—to keep thee living.

[Sings in Gonzalo's ear]
While you here do snoring lie,
Open-ey'd Conspiracy
His time doth take.
If of life you keep a care,
Shake off slumber, and beware.
Awake! awake!

ANTONIO
Then let us both be sudden.

GONZALO
Now, good angels
Preserve the King!

[They wake]

ALONSO
Why, how now! Ho, awake! Why are you drawn?
Wherefore this ghastly looking?

GONZALO
What's the matter?

SEBASTIAN
Whiles we stood here securing your repose,
Even now, we heard a hollow burst of bellowing
Like bulls, or rather lions; did't not wake you?
It struck mine ear most terribly.

ALONSO
I heard nothing.

ANTONIO
O! 'twas a din to fright a monster's ear,
To make an earthquake: sure it was the roar
Of a whole herd of lions.

ALONSO
Heard you this, Gonzalo?

GONZALO
Upon mine honour, sir, I heard a humming,
And that a strange one too, which did awake me.
I shak'd you, sir, and cried; as mine eyes open'd,
I saw their weapons drawn:—there was a noise,
That's verily. 'Tis best we stand upon our guard,
Or that we quit this place: let's draw our weapons.

ALONSO
Lead off this ground: and let's make further search
For my poor son.

GONZALO
Heavens keep him from these beasts!
For he is, sure, i' th' island.

ALONSO
Lead away.

[Exit with the others.]

ARIEL
Prospero my lord shall know what I have done:
So, King, go safely on to seek thy son.

[Exit]

Scene II. Another part of the island

[Enter Caliban, with a burden of wood. A noise of thunder heard]

CALIBAN
All the infections that the sun sucks up
From bogs, fens, flats, on Prosper fall, and make him
By inch-meal a disease! His spirits hear me,
And yet I needs must curse. But they'll nor pinch,
Fright me with urchin-shows, pitch me i' the mire,
Nor lead me, like a firebrand, in the dark
Out of my way, unless he bid 'em; but
For every trifle are they set upon me:
Sometime like apes that mow and chatter at me,
And after bite me; then like hedge-hogs which
Lie tumbling in my bare-foot way, and mount
Their pricks at my foot-fall; sometime am I
All wound with adders, who with cloven tongues
Do hiss me into madness.—

[Enter Trinculo]

Lo, now, lo!
Here comes a spirit of his, and to torment me
For bringing wood in slowly. I'll fall flat;
Perchance he will not mind me.

TRINCULO
Here's neither bush nor shrub to bear off any weather at all, and
another storm brewing; I hear it sing i' th' wind; yond same black
cloud, yond huge one, looks like a foul bombard that would shed
his liquor. If it should thunder as it did before, I know not where
to hide my head: yond same cloud cannot choose but fall by
pailfuls.—What have we here? a man or a fish? dead or alive? A
fish: he smells like a fish: a very ancient and fish-like smell; a kind
of not of the newest Poor-John. A strange fish! Were I in England

now,—as once I was, and had but this fish painted, not a holiday
fool there but would give a piece of silver: there would this monster make a man; any strange beast there makes a man. When
they will not give a doit to relieve a lame beggar, they will lay
out ten to see a dead Indian. Legg'd like a man, and his fins like
arms! Warm, o' my troth! I do now let loose my opinion: hold it
no longer; this is no fish, but an islander, that hath lately suffered
by thunderbolt. *[Thunder]* Alas, the storm is come again! My best
way is to creep under his gaberdine; there is no other shelter here-
about: misery acquaints a man with strange bed-fellows. I will
here shroud till the dregs of the storm be past.

[Enter Stephano singing; a bottle in his hand]

STEPHANO
I shall no more to sea, to sea,
Here shall I die a-shore:—

This is a very scurvy tune to sing at a man's funeral:
Well, here's my comfort.

[Drinks]

The master, the swabber, the boatswain, and I,
The gunner, and his mate,
Lov'd Mall, Meg, and Marian, and Margery,
But none of us car'd for Kate:
For she had a tongue with a tang,
Would cry to a sailor 'Go hang!'
She lov'd not the savour of tar nor of pitch,
Yet a tailor might scratch her wher-e'er she did itch.
Then to sea, boys, and let her go hang.

This is a scurvy tune too: but here's my comfort.

[Drinks]

CALIBAN
Do not torment me: O!

STEPHANO
What's the matter? Have we devils here? Do you put tricks upon
us with savages and men of Ind? Ha! I have not 'scaped drowning, to be afeard now of your four legs; for it hath been said, As
proper a man as ever went on four legs cannot make him give
ground: and it shall be said so again, while Stephano breathes at
's nostrils.

CALIBAN
The spirit torments me: O!

STEPHANO
This is some monster of the isle with four legs, who hath got, as I
take it, an ague. Where the devil should he learn our language? I
will give him some relief, if it be but for that; if I can recover him
and keep him tame and get to Naples with him, he's a present for
any emperor that ever trod on neat's-leather.

CALIBAN
Do not torment me, prithee; I'll bring my wood home faster.

STEPHANO
He's in his fit now and does not talk after the wisest. He shall taste
of my bottle: if he have never drunk wine afore, it will go near to
remove his fit. If I can recover him, and keep him tame, I will not
take too much for him: he shall pay for him that hath him, and
that soundly.

CALIBAN
Thou dost me yet but little hurt; thou wilt anon,
I know it by thy trembling: now Prosper works upon thee.

STEPHANO

Come on your ways: open your mouth; here is that which will give language to you, cat. Open your mouth: this will shake your shaking, I can tell you, and that soundly *[gives Caliban a drink]*: you cannot tell who's your friend: open your chaps again.

TRINCULO

I should know that voice: it should be—but he is drowned; and these are devils. O! defend me.

STEPHANO

Four legs and two voices; a most delicate monster! His forward voice now is to speak well of his friend; his backward voice is to utter foul speeches, and to detract. If all the wine in my bottle will recover him, I will help his ague. Come. Amen! I will pour some in thy other mouth.

TRINCULO

Stephano!

STEPHANO

Doth thy other mouth call me? Mercy! mercy!
This is a devil, and no monster: I will leave him: I
have no long spoon.

TRINCULO

Stephano!—If thou beest Stephano, touch me, and speak to me; for I am Trinculo:—be not afeared—thy good friend Trinculo.

STEPHANO

If thou beest Trinculo, come forth. I'll pull thee by the lesser legs: if any be Trinculo's legs, these are they. Thou art very Trinculo indeed! How cam'st thou to be the siege of this moon-calf? Can he vent Trinculos?

TRINCULO
I took him to be kill'd with a thunderstroke. But art thou not drown'd, Stephano? I hope now thou are not drown'd. Is the storm overblown? I hid me under the dead moon-calf's gaberdine for fear of the storm. And art thou living, Stephano? O Stephano, two Neapolitans 'scaped!

STEPHANO
Prithee, do not turn me about: my stomach is not constant.

CALIBAN
[Aside] These be fine things, an if they be not sprites.
That's a brave god, and bears celestial liquor;
I will kneel to him.

STEPHANO
How didst thou 'scape? How cam'st thou hither? swear by this bottle how thou cam'st hither—I escaped upon a butt of sack, which the sailors heaved overboard, by this bottle! which I made of the bark of a tree, with mine own hands, since I was cast ashore.

CALIBAN
I'll swear upon that bottle to be thy true subject, for the liquor is not earthly.

STEPHANO
Here: swear then how thou escapedst.

TRINCULO
Swum ashore, man, like a duck: I can swim like a duck, I'll be sworn.

STEPHANO
[Passing the bottle] Here, kiss the book [gives
TRINCULO a drink]. Though thou canst swim like a
duck, thou art made like a goose.

TRINCULO
O Stephano! hast any more of this?

STEPHANO
The whole butt, man: my cellar is in a rock by
the seaside, where my wine is hid. How now, moon-calf!
How does thine ague?

CALIBAN
Hast thou not dropped from heaven?

STEPHANO
Out o' the moon, I do assure thee: I was the Man in the Moon,
when time was.

CALIBAN
I have seen thee in her, and I do adore thee, my mistress showed
me thee, and thy dog and thy bush.

STEPHANO
Come, swear to that; kiss the book; I will furnish it anon with
new contents; swear.

TRINCULO
By this good light, this is a very shallow monster.—I afeard of
him!—A very weak monster. —The Man i' the Moon! A most
poor credulous monster!—Well drawn, monster, in good sooth!

CALIBAN
I'll show thee every fertile inch o' the island;
And I will kiss thy foot. I prithee, be my god.

TRINCULO
By this light, a most perfidious and drunken monster: when his
god's asleep, he'll rob his bottle.

CALIBAN
I'll kiss thy foot: I'll swear myself thy subject.

STEPHANO
Come on, then; down, and swear.

TRINCULO
I shall laugh myself to death at this puppy-headed monster.
A most scurvy monster! I could find in my heart to beat him,—

STEPHANO
Come, kiss.

TRINCULO
But that the poor monster's in drink: an abominable monster!

CALIBAN
I'll show thee the best springs; I'll pluck thee berries;
I'll fish for thee, and get thee wood enough.
A plague upon the tyrant that I serve!
I'll bear him no more sticks, but follow thee,
Thou wondrous man.

TRINCULO
A most ridiculous monster, to make a wonder of a poor drunkard!

CALIBAN
I prithee, let me bring thee where crabs grow;
And I with my long nails will dig thee pig-nuts;
Show thee a jay's nest, and instruct thee how
To snare the nimble marmozet; I'll bring thee
To clust'ring filberts, and sometimes I'll get thee
Young scamels from the rock. Wilt thou go with me?

STEPHANO
I prithee now, lead the way without any more talking—Trinculo,
the king and all our company else being drowned, we will inherit

here.—Here, bear my bottle.—Fellow Trinculo, we'll fill him by and by again.

CALIBAN
Farewell, master; farewell, farewell! *[Sings drunkenly]*

TRINCULO
A howling monster, a drunken monster.

CALIBAN
No more dams I'll make for fish;
Nor fetch in firing
At requiring,
Nor scrape trenchering, nor wash dish;
'Ban 'Ban, Ca—Caliban,
Has a new master—Get a new man.
Freedom, high-day! high-day, freedom! freedom,
high-day, freedom!

STEPHANO
O brave monster! lead the way.

[Exeunt]

ACT III

Scene I. Before Prospero's cell

[Enter Ferdinand, bearing a log.]

FERDINAND
There be some sports are painful, and their labour
Delight in them sets off: some kinds of baseness
Are nobly undergone, and most poor matters
Point to rich ends. This my mean task
Would be as heavy to me as odious; but

The mistress which I serve quickens what's dead,
And makes my labours pleasures: O! she is
Ten times more gentle than her father's crabbed,
And he's compos'd of harshness. I must remove
Some thousands of these logs, and pile them up,
Upon a sore injunction: my sweet mistress
Weeps when she sees me work, and says such baseness
Had never like executor. I forget:
But these sweet thoughts do even refresh my labours,
Most busy, least when I do it.

[Enter Miranda, and Prospero behind.]

MIRANDA
Alas! now pray you,
Work not so hard: I would the lightning had
Burnt up those logs that you are enjoin'd to pile!
Pray, set it down and rest you: when this burns,
'Twill weep for having wearied you. My father
Is hard at study; pray, now, rest yourself:
He's safe for these three hours.

FERDINAND
O most dear mistress,
The sun will set, before I shall discharge
What I must strive to do.

MIRANDA
If you'll sit down,
I'll bear your logs the while. Pray give me that;
I'll carry it to the pile.

FERDINAND
No, precious creature:
I had rather crack my sinews, break my back,
Than you should such dishonour undergo,
While I sit lazy by.

MIRANDA
It would become me
As well as it does you: and I should do it
With much more ease; for my good will is to it,
And yours it is against.

PROSPERO
[Aside] Poor worm! thou art infected:
This visitation shows it.

MIRANDA
You look wearily.

FERDINAND
No, noble mistress; 'tis fresh morning with me
When you are by at night. I do beseech you—
Chiefly that I might set it in my prayers—
What is your name?

MIRANDA
Miranda—O my father!
I have broke your hest to say so.

FERDINAND
Admir'd Miranda!
Indeed, the top of admiration; worth
What's dearest to the world! Full many a lady
I have ey'd with best regard, and many a time
The harmony of their tongues hath into bondage
Brought my too diligent ear: for several virtues
Have I lik'd several women; never any
With so full soul but some defect in her
Did quarrel with the noblest grace she ow'd,
And put it to the foil: but you, O you!
So perfect and so peerless, are created
Of every creature's best.

MIRANDA
I do not know
One of my sex; no woman's face remember,
Save, from my glass, mine own; nor have I seen
More that I may call men than you, good friend,
And my dear father: how features are abroad,
I am skill-less of; but, by my modesty,—
The jewel in my dower,—I would not wish
Any companion in the world but you;
Nor can imagination form a shape,
Besides yourself, to like of. But I prattle
Something too wildly, and my father's precepts
I therein do forget.

FERDINAND
I am, in my condition,
A prince, Miranda; I do think, a king;—
I would not so!—and would no more endure
This wooden slavery than to suffer
The flesh-fly blow my mouth.—Hear my soul speak:—
The very instant that I saw you, did
My heart fly to your service; there resides,
To make me slave to it; and for your sake
Am I this patient log-man.

MIRANDA
Do you love me?

FERDINAND
O heaven! O earth! bear witness to this sound,
And crown what I profess with kind event,
If I speak true: if hollowly, invert
What best is boded me to mischief! I,
Beyond all limit of what else i' the world,
Do love, prize, honour you.

MIRANDA
I am a fool
To weep at what I am glad of.

PROSPERO
[Aside] Fair encounter
Of two most rare affections! Heavens rain grace
On that which breeds between them!

FERDINAND
Wherefore weep you?

MIRANDA
At mine unworthiness, that dare not offer
What I desire to give; and much less take
What I shall die to want. But this is trifling;
And all the more it seeks to hide itself,
The bigger bulk it shows. Hence, bashful cunning!
And prompt me, plain and holy innocence!
I am your wife, if you will marry me;
If not, I'll die your maid: to be your fellow
You may deny me; but I'll be your servant,
Whether you will or no.

FERDINAND
My mistress, dearest;
And I thus humble ever.

MIRANDA
My husband, then?

FERDINAND
Ay, with a heart as willing
As bondage e'er of freedom: here's my hand.

MIRANDA
And mine, with my heart in't: and now farewell
Till half an hour hence.

FERDINAND
A thousand thousand!

[Exeunt Ferdinand and Miranda severally.]

PROSPERO
So glad of this as they, I cannot be,
Who are surpris'd withal; but my rejoicing
At nothing can be more. I'll to my book;
For yet, ere supper time, must I perform
Much business appertaining.

[Exit]

Scene II. Another part of the island

[Enter Caliban, with a bottle, Stephano, and Trinculo]

STEPHANO
Tell not me:—when the butt is out we will drink water; not a
drop before: therefore bear up, and board 'em.—Servant-monster,
drink to me.

TRINCULO
Servant-monster! The folly of this island! They say there's but five
upon this isle; we are three of them; if th' other two be brained
like us, the state totters.

STEPHANO
Drink, servant-monster, when I bid thee: thy eyes are almost set
in thy head.

TRINCULO
Where should they be set else? He were a brave monster indeed,
if they were set in his tail.

STEPHANO
My man-monster hath drown'd his tongue in sack: for my part,
the sea cannot drown me; I swam, ere I could recover the shore,
five-and-thirty leagues, off and on, by this light. Thou shalt be my
lieutenant, monster, or my standard.

TRINCULO
Your lieutenant, if you list; he's no standard.

STEPHANO
We'll not run, Monsieur monster.

TRINCULO
Nor go neither: but you'll lie like dogs, and yet say nothing neither.

STEPHANO
Moon-calf, speak once in thy life, if thou beest a good moon-calf.

CALIBAN
How does thy honour? Let me lick thy shoe.
I'll not serve him: he is not valiant.

TRINCULO
Thou liest, most ignorant monster: I am in case to justle a con-
stable. Why, thou deboshed fish thou, was there ever man a cow-
ard that hath drunk so much sack as I to-day? Wilt thou tell a
monstrous lie, being but half fish and half a monster?

CALIBAN
Lo, how he mocks me! wilt thou let him, my lord?

TRINCULO
'Lord' quoth he!—That a monster should be such a natural!

CALIBAN
Lo, lo again! bite him to death, I prithee.

STEPHANO
Trinculo, keep a good tongue in your head: if you prove a muti-
neer, the next tree! The poor monster's my subject, and he shall
not suffer indignity.

CALIBAN
I thank my noble lord. Wilt thou be pleas'd to hearken once again
to the suit I made to thee?

STEPHANO
Marry will I; kneel, and repeat it: I will stand, and so shall Trinculo.

[Enter Ariel, invisible]

CALIBAN
As I told thee before, I am subject to a tyrant, sorcerer, that by his
cunning hath cheated me of the island.

ARIEL
Thou liest.

CALIBAN
Thou liest, thou jesting monkey, thou;
I would my valiant master would destroy thee;
I do not lie.

STEPHANO
Trinculo, if you trouble him any more in his tale, by this hand, I
will supplant some of your teeth.

TRINCULO
Why, I said nothing.

STEPHANO
Mum, then, and no more.—*[To Caliban]* Proceed.

CALIBAN
I say, by sorcery he got this isle;
From me he got it: if thy greatness will ,
Revenge it on him,—for I know, thou dar'st;
But this thing dare not,—

STEPHANO
That's most certain.

CALIBAN
Thou shalt be lord of it and I'll serve thee.

STEPHANO
How now shall this be compassed? Canst thou bring me to the party?

CALIBAN
Yea, yea, my lord: I'll yield him thee asleep,
Where thou may'st knock a nail into his head.

ARIEL
Thou liest: thou canst not.

CALIBAN
What a pied ninny's this! Thou scurvy patch!—
I do beseech thy greatness, give him blows,
And take his bottle from him: when that's gone
He shall drink nought but brine; for I'll not show him
Where the quick freshes are.

STEPHANO
Trinculo, run into no further danger: interrupt the monster one word further and, by this hand, I'll turn my mercy out o' doors, and make a stock-fish of thee.

TRINCULO
Why, what did I? I did nothing. I'll go farther off.

STEPHANO
Didst thou not say he lied?

ARIEL
Thou liest.

STEPHANO
Do I so? Take thou that. *[Strikes Trinculo]* As you like this, give me the lie another time.

TRINCULO
I did not give the lie:—out o' your wits and hearing too?—A pox o' your bottle! this can sack and drinking do.—A murrain on your monster, and the devil take your fingers!

CALIBAN
Ha, ha, ha!

STEPHANO
Now, forward with your tale.—Prithee stand further off.

CALIBAN
Beat him enough: after a little time, I'll beat him too.

STEPHANO
Stand farther.—Come, proceed.

CALIBAN
Why, as I told thee, 'tis a custom with him
I' th' afternoon to sleep: there thou may'st brain him,
Having first seiz'd his books; or with a log
Batter his skull, or paunch him with a stake,
Or cut his wezand with thy knife. Remember

First to possess his books; for without them
He's but a sot, as I am, nor hath not
One spirit to command: they all do hate him
As rootedly as I. Burn but his books;
He has brave utensils,—for so he calls them,—
Which, when he has a house, he'll deck withal:
And that most deeply to consider is
The beauty of his daughter; he himself
Calls her a nonpareil: I never saw a woman
But only Sycorax my dam and she;
But she as far surpasseth Sycorax
As great'st does least.

STEPHANO
Is it so brave a lass?

CALIBAN
Ay, lord: she will become thy bed, I warrant,
And bring thee forth brave brood.

STEPHANO
Monster, I will kill this man; his daughter and I will be king and
queen,—save our graces!—and Trinculo and thyself shall be vice-
roys. Dost thou like the plot, Trinculo?

TRINCULO
Excellent.

STEPHANO
Give me thy hand: I am sorry I beat thee; but while thou livest,
keep a good tongue in thy head.

CALIBAN
Within this half hour will he be asleep;
Wilt thou destroy him then?

STEPHANO
Ay, on mine honour.

ARIEL
This will I tell my master.

CALIBAN
Thou mak'st me merry: I am full of pleasure.
Let us be jocund: will you troll the catch
You taught me but while-ere?

STEPHANO
At thy request, monster, I will do reason, any reason. Come on,
Trinculo, let us sing.

[Sings]

Flout 'em and scout 'em; and scout 'em and flout 'em:
Thought is free.

CALIBAN
That's not the tune.

[Ariel plays the tune on a Tabor and Pipe.]

STEPHANO
What is this same?

TRINCULO
This is the tune of our catch, played by the picture of Nobody.

STEPHANO
If thou beest a man, show thyself in thy likeness: if thou beest a
devil, take't as thou list.

TRINCULO
O, forgive me my sins!

STEPHANO
He that dies pays all debts: I defy thee.—Mercy upon us!

CALIBAN
Art thou afeard?

STEPHANO
No, monster, not I.

CALIBAN
Be not afeard: the isle is full of noises,
Sounds, and sweet airs, that give delight, and hurt not.
Sometimes a thousand twangling instruments
Will hum about mine ears; and sometimes voices,
That, if I then had wak'd after long sleep,
Will make me sleep again: and then, in dreaming,
The clouds methought would open and show riches
Ready to drop upon me; that, when I wak'd,
I cried to dream again.

STEPHANO
This will prove a brave kingdom to me, where I shall have my
music for nothing.

CALIBAN
When Prospero is destroyed.

STEPHANO
That shall be by and by: I remember the story.

TRINCULO
The sound is going away: let's follow it, and after do our work.

STEPHANO
Lead, monster: we'll follow.—I would I could see this taborer! he
lays it on. Wilt come?

TRINCULO
I'll follow, Stephano.

[Exeunt]

Scene III. Another part of the island

[Enter Alonso, Sebastian, Antonio, Gonzalo, Adrian, Francisco, and Others.]

GONZALO
By'r lakin, I can go no further, sir;
My old bones ache: here's a maze trod, indeed,
Through forth-rights and meanders! By your patience,
I needs must rest me.

ALONSO
Old lord, I cannot blame thee,
Who am myself attach'd with weariness
To th' dulling of my spirits: sit down, and rest.
Even here I will put off my hope, and keep it
No longer for my flatterer: he is drown'd
Whom thus we stray to find; and the sea mocks
Our frustrate search on land. Well, let him go.

ANTONIO
[Aside to Sebastian] I am right glad that he's
so out of hope.
Do not, for one repulse, forgo the purpose
That you resolv'd to effect.

SEBASTIAN
[Aside to Antonio] The next advantage
Will we take throughly.

ANTONIO
[Aside to Sebastian] Let it be to-night;
For, now they are oppress'd with travel, they
Will not, nor cannot, use such vigilance
As when they are fresh.

Sebastian
[Aside to Antonio] I say, to-night: no more.

[Solemn and strange music: and Prospero above, invisible. Enter several strange Shapes, bringing in a banquet: they dance about it with gentle actions of salutation; and inviting the King, etc., to eat, they depart.]

Alonso
What harmony is this? my good friends, hark!

Gonzalo
Marvellous sweet music!

Alonso
Give us kind keepers, heavens! What were these?

Sebastian
A living drollery. Now I will believe
That there are unicorns; that in Arabia
There is one tree, the phoenix' throne; one phoenix
At this hour reigning there.

Antonio
I'll believe both;
And what does else want credit, come to me,
And I'll be sworn 'tis true: travellers ne'er did lie,
Though fools at home condemn them.

Gonzalo
If in Naples
I should report this now, would they believe me?
If I should say, I saw such islanders,—
For, certes, these are people of the island,—
Who, though, they are of monstrous shape, yet, note,
Their manners are more gentle-kind than of
Our human generation you shall find
Many, nay, almost any.

PROSPERO
[Aside] Honest lord,
Thou hast said well; for some of you there present
Are worse than devils.

ALONSO
I cannot too much muse
Such shapes, such gesture, and such sound, expressing,—
Although they want the use of tongue,—a kind
Of excellent dumb discourse.

PROSPERO
[Aside] Praise in departing.

FRANCISCO
They vanish'd strangely.

SEBASTIAN
No matter, since
They have left their viands behind; for we have stomachs.—
Will't please you taste of what is here?

ALONSO
Not I.

GONZALO
Faith, sir, you need not fear. When we were boys,
Who would believe that there were mountaineers
Dewlapp'd like bulls, whose throats had hanging at them
Wallets of flesh? or that there were such men
Whose heads stood in their breasts? which now we find
Each putter-out of five for one will bring us
Good warrant of.

ALONSO
I will stand to, and feed,
Although my last; no matter, since I feel

The best is past.—Brother, my lord the duke,
Stand to and do as we.

[Thunder and lightning. Enter Ariel, like a harpy; claps his wings
upon the table; and, with a quaint device, the banquet vanishes]

ARIEL
You are three men of sin, whom Destiny,
That hath to instrument this lower world
And what is in't,—the never-surfeited sea
Hath caused to belch up you; and on this island
Where man doth not inhabit; you 'mongst men
Being most unfit to live. I have made you mad:

[Seeing Alonso, Sebastian, etc., draw their swords]

And even with such-like valour men hang and drown
Their proper selves. You fools! I and my fellows
Are ministers of fate: the elements
Of whom your swords are temper'd may as well
Wound the loud winds, or with bemock'd-at stabs
Kill the still-closing waters, as diminish
One dowle that's in my plume; my fellow-ministers
Are like invulnerable. If you could hurt,
Your swords are now too massy for your strengths,
And will not be uplifted. But, remember—
For that's my business to you,—that you three
From Milan did supplant good Prospero;
Expos'd unto the sea, which hath requit it,
Him, and his innocent child: for which foul deed
The powers, delaying, not forgetting, have
Incens'd the seas and shores, yea, all the creatures,
Against your peace. Thee of thy son, Alonso,
They have bereft; and do pronounce, by me
Lingering perdition,—worse than any death
Can be at once,—shall step by step attend

You and your ways; whose wraths to guard you from—
Which here, in this most desolate isle, else falls
Upon your heads,—is nothing but heart-sorrow,
And a clear life ensuing.

*[He vanishes in thunder: then, to soft music, enter the Shapes again,
and dance, with mocks and mows, and carry out the table]*

PROSPERO
[Aside] Bravely the figure of this harpy hast thou
Perform'd, my Ariel; a grace it had, devouring;
Of my instruction hast thou nothing bated
In what thou hadst to say: so, with good life
And observation strange, my meaner ministers
Their several kinds have done. My high charms work,
And these mine enemies are all knit up
In their distractions; they now are in my power;
And in these fits I leave them, while I visit
Young Ferdinand,—whom they suppose is drown'd,—
And his and mine lov'd darling.

[Exit above]

GONZALO
I' the name of something holy, sir, why stand you
In this strange stare?

ALONSO
O, it is monstrous! monstrous!
Methought the billows spoke, and told me of it;
The winds did sing it to me; and the thunder,
That deep and dreadful organ-pipe, pronounc'd
The name of Prosper: it did bass my trespass.
Therefore my son i' th' ooze is bedded; and
I'll seek him deeper than e'er plummet sounded,
And with him there lie mudded.

[Exit]

SEBASTIAN
But one fiend at a time,
I'll fight their legions o'er.

ANTONIO
I'll be thy second.

[Exeunt Sebastian and Antonio]

GONZALO
All three of them are desperate: their great guilt,
Like poison given to work a great time after,
Now 'gins to bite the spirits. I do beseech you
That are of suppler joints, follow them swiftly
And hinder them from what this ecstasy
May now provoke them to.

ADRIAN
Follow, I pray you.

[Exeunt]

ACT IV

Scene 1. Before Prospero's cell

[Enter Prospero, Ferdinand, and Miranda]

PROSPERO
If I have too austerely punish'd you,
Your compensation makes amends: for
Have given you here a third of mine own life,
Or that for which I live; who once again
I tender to thy hand: all thy vexations

Were but my trials of thy love, and thou
Hast strangely stood the test: here, afore Heaven,
I ratify this my rich gift. O Ferdinand!
Do not smile at me that I boast her off,
For thou shalt find she will outstrip all praise,
And make it halt behind her.

FERDINAND
I do believe it
Against an oracle.

PROSPERO
Then, as my gift and thine own acquisition
Worthily purchas'd, take my daughter: but
If thou dost break her virgin knot before
All sanctimonious ceremonies may
With full and holy rite be minister'd,
No sweet aspersion shall the heavens let fall
To make this contract grow; but barren hate,
Sour-ey'd disdain, and discord, shall bestrew
The union of your bed with weeds so loathly
That you shall hate it both: therefore take heed,
As Hymen's lamps shall light you.

FERDINAND
As I hope
For quiet days, fair issue, and long life,
With such love as 'tis now, the murkiest den,
The most opportune place, the strong'st suggestion
Our worser genius can, shall never melt
Mine honour into lust, to take away
The edge of that day's celebration,
When I shall think, or Phoebus' steeds are founder'd,
Or Night kept chain'd below.

PROSPERO
Fairly spoke:
Sit, then, and talk with her, she is thine own.
What, Ariel! my industrious servant, Ariel!

[Enter Ariel]

ARIEL
What would my potent master? here I am.

PROSPERO
Thou and thy meaner fellows your last service
Did worthily perform; and I must use you
In such another trick. Go bring the rabble,
O'er whom I give thee power, here to this place;
Incite them to quick motion; for I must
Bestow upon the eyes of this young couple
Some vanity of mine art: it is my promise,
And they expect it from me.

ARIEL
Presently?

PROSPERO
Ay, with a twink.

ARIEL
Before you can say 'Come' and 'Go,'
And breathe twice; and cry 'so, so,'
Each one, tripping on his toe,
Will be here with mop and mow.
Do you love me, master? no?

PROSPERO
Dearly, my delicate Ariel. Do not approach
Till thou dost hear me call.

ARIEL
Well, I conceive.

[Exit]

PROSPERO
Look, thou be true; do not give dalliance
Too much the rein: the strongest oaths are straw
To th' fire i' the blood: be more abstemious,
Or else good night your vow!

FERDINAND
I warrant you, sir;
The white-cold virgin snow upon my heart
Abates the ardour of my liver.

PROSPERO
Well.—
Now come, my Ariel! bring a corollary,
Rather than want a spirit: appear, and pertly.
No tongue! all eyes! be silent.

[Soft music]

[A Masque. Enter Iris]

IRIS
Ceres, most bounteous lady, thy rich leas
Of wheat, rye, barley, vetches, oats, and peas;
Thy turfy mountains, where live nibbling sheep,
And flat meads thatch'd with stover, them to keep;
Thy banks with pioned and twilled brims,
Which spongy April at thy hest betrims,
To make cold nymphs chaste crowns; and thy broom groves,
Whose shadow the dismissed bachelor loves,
Being lass-lorn: thy pole-clipt vineyard;

And thy sea-marge, sterile and rocky-hard,
Where thou thyself dost air: the Queen o' the sky,
Whose watery arch and messenger am I,
Bids thee leave these; and with her sovereign grace,
Here on this grass-plot, in this very place,
To come and sport; her peacocks fly amain:
Approach, rich Ceres, her to entertain.

[Enter Ceres]

CERES
Hail, many-colour'd messenger, that ne'er
Dost disobey the wife of Jupiter;
Who with thy saffron wings upon my flowers
Diffusest honey drops, refreshing showers:
And with each end of thy blue bow dost crown
My bosky acres and my unshrubb'd down,
Rich scarf to my proud earth; why hath thy queen
Summon'd me hither to this short-grass'd green?

IRIS
A contract of true love to celebrate,
And some donation freely to estate
On the blest lovers.

CERES
Tell me, heavenly bow,
If Venus or her son, as thou dost know,
Do now attend the queen? Since they did plot
The means that dusky Dis my daughter got,
Her and her blind boy's scandal'd company
I have forsworn.

IRIS
Of her society
Be not afraid. I met her deity

Cutting the clouds towards Paphos and her son
Dove-drawn with her. Here thought they to have done
Some wanton charm upon this man and maid,
Whose vows are, that no bed-rite shall be paid
Till Hymen's torch be lighted; but in vain.
Mars's hot minion is return'd again;
Her waspish-headed son has broke his arrows,
Swears he will shoot no more, but play with sparrows,
And be a boy right out.

CERES
Highest Queen of State,
Great Juno comes; I know her by her gait.

[Enter Juno]

JUNO
How does my bounteous sister? Go with me
To bless this twain, that they may prosperous be,
And honour'd in their issue.

SONG

JUNO
Honour, riches, marriage-blessing,
Long continuance, and increasing,
Hourly joys be still upon you!
Juno sings her blessings on you.

CERES
Earth's increase, foison plenty,
Barns and gamers never empty;
Vines with clust'ring bunches growing;
Plants with goodly burden bowing;
Spring come to you at the farthest,
In the very end of harvest!
Scarcity and want shall shun you;
Ceres' blessing so is on you.

FERDINAND
This is a most majestic vision, and
Harmonious charmingly; may I be bold
To think these spirits?

PROSPERO
Spirits, which by mine art
I have from their confines call'd to enact
My present fancies.

FERDINAND
Let me live here ever:
So rare a wonder'd father and a wise,
Makes this place Paradise.

[Juno and Ceres whisper, and send Iris on employment.]

PROSPERO
Sweet now, silence!
Juno and Ceres whisper seriously,
There's something else to do: hush, and be mute,
Or else our spell is marr'd.

IRIS
You nymphs, call'd Naiads, of the windring brooks,
With your sedg'd crowns and ever-harmless looks,
Leave your crisp channels, and on this green land
Answer your summons: Juno does command.
Come, temperate nymphs, and help to celebrate
A contract of true love: be not too late.

[Enter certain Nymphs]

You sun-burn'd sicklemen, of August weary,
Come hither from the furrow, and be merry:
Make holiday: your rye-straw hats put on,
And these fresh nymphs encounter every one
In country footing.

[Enter certain Reapers, properly habited: they join with the Nymphs in a graceful dance; towards the end whereof Prospero starts suddenly, and speaks; after which, to a strange, hollow, and confused noise, they heavily vanish.]

PROSPERO
[Aside] I had forgot that foul conspiracy
Of the beast Caliban and his confederates
Against my life: the minute of their plot
Is almost come. *[To the Spirits.]* Well done! avoid; no more!

FERDINAND
This is strange: your father's in some passion
That works him strongly.

MIRANDA
Never till this day
Saw I him touch'd with anger so distemper'd.

PROSPERO
You do look, my son, in a mov'd sort,
As if you were dismay'd: be cheerful, sir:
Our revels now are ended. These our actors,
As I foretold you, were all spirits and
Are melted into air, into thin air:
And, like the baseless fabric of this vision,
The cloud-capp'd towers, the gorgeous palaces,
The solemn temples, the great globe itself,
Yea, all which it inherit, shall dissolve
And, like this insubstantial pageant faded,
Leave not a rack behind. We are such stuff
As dreams are made on, and our little life
Is rounded with a sleep.—Sir, I am vex'd:
Bear with my weakness; my old brain is troubled.
Be not disturb'd with my infirmity.
If you be pleas'd, retire into my cell

And there repose: a turn or two I'll walk,
To still my beating mind.

FERDINAND, MIRANDA
We wish your peace.

[Exeunt.]

PROSPERO
Come, with a thought.—*[To them.]* I thank thee:
Ariel, come!

[Enter Ariel]

ARIEL
Thy thoughts I cleave to. What's thy pleasure?

PROSPERO
Spirit,
We must prepare to meet with Caliban.

ARIEL
Ay, my commander; when I presented Ceres,
I thought to have told thee of it: but I fear'd
Lest I might anger thee.

PROSPERO
Say again, where didst thou leave these varlets?

ARIEL
I told you, sir, they were red-hot with drinking;
So full of valour that they smote the air
For breathing in their faces; beat the ground
For kissing of their feet; yet always bending
Towards their project. Then I beat my tabor;
At which, like unback'd colts, they prick'd their ears,

Advanc'd their eyelids, lifted up their noses
As they smelt music: so I charm'd their ears,
That calf-like they my lowing follow'd through
Tooth'd briers, sharp furzes, pricking goss and thorns,
Which enter'd their frail shins: at last I left them
I' the filthy-mantled pool beyond your cell,
There dancing up to the chins, that the foul lake
O'erstunk their feet.

PROSPERO
This was well done, my bird.
Thy shape invisible retain thou still:
The trumpery in my house, go bring it hither
For stale to catch these thieves.

ARIEL
I go, I go.

[Exit]

PROSPERO
A devil, a born devil, on whose nature
Nurture can never stick; on whom my pains,
Humanely taken, all, all lost, quite lost;
And as with age his body uglier grows,
So his mind cankers. I will plague them all,
Even to roaring.

[Re-enter Ariel, loaden with glistering apparel, etc.]

Come, hang them on this line.

[Prospero and Ariel remain invisible. Enter Caliban, Stephano,
and Trinculo, all wet]

CALIBAN
Pray you, tread softly, that the blind mole may not
Hear a foot fall: we now are near his cell.

STEPHANO
Monster, your fairy, which you say is a harmless
fairy, has done little better than played the
Jack with us.

TRINCULO
Monster, I do smell all horse-piss; at which my nose is in great
indignation.

STEPHANO
So is mine.—Do you hear, monster? If I should take a displeasure
against you, look you,—

TRINCULO
Thou wert but a lost monster.

CALIBAN
Good my lord, give me thy favour still:
Be patient, for the prize I'll bring thee to
Shall hoodwink this mischance: therefore speak softly;
All's hush'd as midnight yet.

TRINCULO
Ay, but to lose our bottles in the pool!—

STEPHANO
There is not only disgrace and dishonour in that, monster, but
an infinite loss.

TRINCULO
That's more to me than my wetting: yet this is your harmless
fairy, monster.

STEPHANO
I will fetch off my bottle, though I be o'er ears for my labour.

CALIBAN
Prithee, my king, be quiet. Seest thou here,
This is the mouth o' the cell: no noise, and enter.
Do that good mischief which may make this island
Thine own for ever, and I, thy Caliban,
For aye thy foot-licker.

STEPHANO
Give me thy hand: I do begin to have bloody thoughts.

TRINCULO
O King Stephano! O peer! O worthy Stephano!
Look what a wardrobe here is for thee!

CALIBAN
Let it alone, thou fool; it is but trash.

TRINCULO
O, ho, monster! we know what belongs to a frippery.—O King
Stephano!

STEPHANO
Put off that gown, Trinculo; by this hand, I'll have that gown.

TRINCULO
Thy Grace shall have it.

CALIBAN
The dropsy drown this fool! What do you mean
To dote thus on such luggage? Let's along,
And do the murder first. If he awake,
From toe to crown he'll fill our skins with pinches;
Make us strange stuff.

STEPHANO
Be you quiet, monster.—Mistress line, is not this my jerkin? Now is the jerkin under the line: now, jerkin, you are like to lose your hair, and prove a bald jerkin.

TRINCULO
Do, do: we steal by line and level, an't like your Grace.

STEPHANO
I thank thee for that jest: here's a garment for't: wit shall not go unrewarded while I am king of this country: 'Steal by line and level,' is an excellent pass of pate: there's another garmet for't.

TRINCULO
Monster, come, put some lime upon your fingers, and away with the rest.

CALIBAN
I will have none on't. We shall lose our time,
And all be turn'd to barnacles, or to apes
With foreheads villainous low.

STEPHANO
Monster, lay-to your fingers: help to bear this away where my hogshead of wine is, or I'll turn you out of my kingdom. Go to; carry this.

TRINCULO
And this.

STEPHANO
Ay, and this.

[A noise of hunters beard. Enter divers Spirits, in shape of hounds, and hunt them about; Prospero and Ariel setting them on]

PROSPERO
Hey, Mountain, hey!

ARIEL
Silver! there it goes, Silver!

PROSPERO
Fury, Fury! There, Tyrant, there! hark, hark!

[Caliban, Stephano, and Trinculo are driven out.]

Go, charge my goblins that they grind their joints
With dry convulsions; shorten up their sinews
With aged cramps, and more pinch-spotted make them
Than pard, or cat o' mountain.

ARIEL
Hark, they roar.

PROSPERO
Let them be hunted soundly. At this hour
Lies at my mercy all mine enemies;
Shortly shall all my labours end, and thou
Shalt have the air at freedom;for a little
Follow, and do me service.

[Exeunt]

ACT V

Scene 1. Before the cell of Prospero

[Enter Prospero in his magic robes; and Ariel]

PROSPERO
Now does my project gather to a head:
My charms crack not; my spirits obey, and time
Goes upright with his carriage. How's the day?

ARIEL
On the sixth hour; at which time, my lord,
You said our work should cease.

PROSPERO
I did say so,
When first I rais'd the tempest. Say, my spirit,
How fares the King and 's followers?

ARIEL
Confin'd together
In the same fashion as you gave in charge;
Just as you left them: all prisoners, sir,
In the line-grove which weather-fends your cell;
They cannot budge till your release. The king,
His brother, and yours, abide all three distracted,
And the remainder mourning over them,
Brim full of sorrow and dismay; but chiefly
Him you term'd, sir, 'the good old lord, Gonzalo':
His tears run down his beard, like winter's drops
From eaves of reeds; your charm so strongly works them,
That if you now beheld them, your affections
Would become tender.

PROSPERO
Dost thou think so, spirit?

ARIEL
Mine would, sir, were I human.

PROSPERO
And mine shall.
Hast thou, which art but air, a touch, a feeling
Of their afflictions, and shall not myself,
One of their kind, that relish all as sharply,
Passion as they, be kindlier mov'd than thou art?

Though with their high wrongs I am struck to the quick,
Yet with my nobler reason 'gainst my fury
Do I take part: the rarer action is
In virtue than in vengeance: they being penitent,
The sole drift of my purpose doth extend
Not a frown further. Go release them, Ariel.
My charms I'll break, their senses I'll restore,
And they shall be themselves.

ARIEL
I'll fetch them, sir.

[Exit.]

PROSPERO
Ye elves of hills, brooks, standing lakes, and groves;
And ye that on the sands with printless foot
Do chase the ebbing Neptune, and do fly him
When he comes back; you demi-puppets that
By moonshine do the green sour ringlets make,
Whereof the ewe not bites; and you whose pastime
Is to make midnight mushrooms, that rejoice
To hear the solemn curfew; by whose aid,—
Weak masters though ye be,—I have bedimm'd
The noontide sun, call'd forth the mutinous winds,
And 'twixt the green sea and the azur'd vault
Set roaring war: to the dread rattling thunder
Have I given fire, and rifted Jove's stout oak
With his own bolt: the strong-bas'd promontory
Have I made shake; and by the spurs pluck'd up
The pine and cedar: graves at my command
Have wak'd their sleepers, op'd, and let them forth
By my so potent art. But this rough magic
I here abjure; and, when I have requir'd
Some heavenly music,—which even now I do,—
To work mine end upon their senses that

This airy charm is for, I'll break my staff,
Bury it certain fathoms in the earth,
And deeper than did ever plummet sound
I'll drown my book.

[Solem music]

[Re-enter Ariel: after him, Alonso, with frantic gesture, attended by Gonzalo; Sebastian and Antonio in like manner, attended by Adrian and Francisco: they all enter the circle which Prospero had made, and there stand charmed: which Prospero observing, speaks.]

A solemn air, and the best comforter
To an unsettled fancy, cure thy brains,
Now useless, boil'd within thy skull! There stand,
For you are spell-stopp'd.
Holy Gonzalo, honourable man,
Mine eyes, even sociable to the show of thine,
Fall fellowly drops. The charm dissolves apace;
And as the morning steals upon the night,
Melting the darkness, so their rising senses
Begin to chase the ignorant fumes that mantle
Their clearer reason.—O good Gonzalo!
My true preserver, and a loyal sir
To him thou follow'st, I will pay thy graces
Home, both in word and deed.—Most cruelly
Didst thou, Alonso, use me and my daughter:
Thy brother was a furtherer in the act;—
Thou'rt pinch'd for't now, Sebastian.—Flesh and blood,
You, brother mine, that entertain'd ambition,
Expell'd remorse and nature, who, with Sebastian,—
Whose inward pinches therefore are most strong,—
Would here have kill'd your king; I do forgive thee,
Unnatural though thou art! Their understanding
Begins to swell, and the approaching tide
Will shortly fill the reasonable shores

That now lie foul and muddy. Not one of them
That yet looks on me, or would know me.—Ariel,
Fetch me the hat and rapier in my cell:—

[Exit Ariel]

I will discase me, and myself present,
As I was sometime Milan.—Quickly, spirit;
Thou shalt ere long be free.

[Ariel re-enters, singing, and helps to attire Prospero]

ARIEL
Where the bee sucks, there suck I:
In a cowslip's bell I lie;
There I couch when owls do cry.
On the bat's back I do fly
After summer merrily:
Merrily, merrily shall I live now
Under the blossom that hangs on the bough.

PROSPERO
Why, that's my dainty Ariel! I shall miss thee;
But yet thou shalt have freedom;—so, so, so.—
To the king's ship, invisible as thou art:
There shalt thou find the mariners asleep
Under the hatches; the master and the boatswain
Being awake, enforce them to this place,
And presently, I prithee.

ARIEL
I drink the air before me, and return
Or ere your pulse twice beat.

[Exit]

GONZALO
All torment, trouble, wonder and amazement
Inhabits here. Some heavenly power guide us
Out of this fearful country!

PROSPERO
Behold, sir king,
The wronged Duke of Milan, Prospero.
For more assurance that a living prince
Does now speak to thee, I embrace thy body;
And to thee and thy company I bid
A hearty welcome.

ALONSO
Whe'er thou be'st he or no,
Or some enchanted trifle to abuse me,
As late I have been, I not know: thy pulse
Beats, as of flesh and blood; and, since I saw thee,
Th' affliction of my mind amends, with which,
I fear, a madness held me: this must crave,—
An if this be at all—a most strange story.
Thy dukedom I resign, and do entreat
Thou pardon me my wrongs.—But how should Prospero
Be living and be here?

PROSPERO
First, noble friend,
Let me embrace thine age; whose honour cannot
Be measur'd or confin'd.

GONZALO
Whether this be
Or be not, I'll not swear.

PROSPERO
You do yet taste
Some subtleties o' the isle, that will not let you

Believe things certain.—Welcome, my friends all:—
[Aside to Sebastian and Antonio] But you, my brace of lords, were I so minded,
I here could pluck his highness' frown upon you,
And justify you traitors: at this time
I will tell no tales.

SEBASTIAN
[Aside] The devil speaks in him.

PROSPERO
No.
For you, most wicked sir, whom to call brother
Would even infect my mouth, I do forgive
Thy rankest fault; all of them; and require
My dukedom of thee, which, perforce, I know
Thou must restore.

ALONSO
If thou beest Prospero,
Give us particulars of thy preservation;
How thou hast met us here, whom three hours since
Were wrack'd upon this shore; where I have lost,—
How sharp the point of this remembrance is!—
My dear son Ferdinand.

PROSPERO
I am woe for't, sir.

ALONSO
Irreparable is the loss, and patience
Says it is past her cure.

PROSPERO
I rather think
You have not sought her help; of whose soft grace,
For the like loss I have her sovereign aid,
And rest myself content.

ALONSO
You the like loss!

PROSPERO
As great to me, as late; and, supportable
To make the dear loss, have I means much weaker
Than you may call to comfort you, for I
Have lost my daughter.

ALONSO
A daughter?
O heavens! that they were living both in Naples,
The king and queen there! That they were, I wish
Myself were mudded in that oozy bed
Where my son lies. When did you lose your daughter?

PROSPERO
In this last tempest. I perceive, these lords
At this encounter do so much admire
That they devour their reason, and scarce think
Their eyes do offices of truth, their words
Are natural breath; but, howsoe'er you have
Been justled from your senses, know for certain
That I am Prospero, and that very duke
Which was thrust forth of Milan; who most strangely
Upon this shore, where you were wrack'd, was landed
To be the lord on't. No more yet of this;
For 'tis a chronicle of day by day,
Not a relation for a breakfast nor
Befitting this first meeting. Welcome, sir:
This cell's my court: here have I few attendants
And subjects none abroad: pray you, look in.
My dukedom since you have given me again,
I will requite you with as good a thing;
At least bring forth a wonder, to content ye
As much as me my dukedom.

[The entrance of the Cell opens, and discovers Ferdinand and Miranda playing at chess.]

MIRANDA
Sweet lord, you play me false.

FERDINAND
No, my dearest love,
I would not for the world.

MIRANDA
Yes, for a score of kingdoms you should wrangle,
And I would call it fair play.

ALONSO
If this prove
A vision of the island, one dear son
Shall I twice lose.

SEBASTIAN
A most high miracle!

FERDINAND
Though the seas threaten, they are merciful:
I have curs'd them without cause.

[Kneels to Alonso]

ALONSO
Now all the blessings
Of a glad father compass thee about!
Arise, and say how thou cam'st here.

MIRANDA
O, wonder!
How many goodly creatures are there here!

How beauteous mankind is! O brave new world
That has such people in't!

PROSPERO
'Tis new to thee.

ALONSO
What is this maid, with whom thou wast at play?
Your eld'st acquaintance cannot be three hours:
Is she the goddess that hath sever'd us,
And brought us thus together?

FERDINAND
Sir, she is mortal;
But by immortal Providence she's mine.
I chose her when I could not ask my father
For his advice, nor thought I had one. She
Is daughter to this famous Duke of Milan,
Of whom so often I have heard renown,
But never saw before; of whom I have
Receiv'd a second life: and second father
This lady makes him to me.

ALONSO
I am hers:
But, O! how oddly will it sound that I
Must ask my child forgiveness!

PROSPERO
There, sir, stop:
Let us not burden our remembrances with
A heaviness that's gone.

GONZALO
I have inly wept,
Or should have spoke ere this. Look down, you gods,

And on this couple drop a blessed crown;
For it is you that have chalk'd forth the way
Which brought us hither.

ALONSO
I say, Amen, Gonzalo!

GONZALO
Was Milan thrust from Milan, that his issue
Should become kings of Naples? O, rejoice
Beyond a common joy, and set it down
With gold on lasting pillars. In one voyage
Did Claribel her husband find at Tunis,
And Ferdinand, her brother, found a wife
Where he himself was lost; Prospero his dukedom
In a poor isle; and all of us ourselves,
When no man was his own.

ALONSO
[To Ferdinand and Miranda] Give me your hands:
Let grief and sorrow still embrace his heart
That doth not wish you joy!

GONZALO
Be it so. Amen!

[Re-enter Ariel, with the Master and Boatswain amazedly following.]

O look, sir! look, sir! Here are more of us.
I prophesied, if a gallows were on land,
This fellow could not drown.—Now, blasphemy,
That swear'st grace o'erboard, not an oath on shore?
Hast thou no mouth by land? What is the news?

BOATSWAIN
The best news is that we have safely found
Our king and company: the next, our ship,—

Which but three glasses since we gave out split,—
Is tight and yare, and bravely rigg'd as when
We first put out to sea.

ARIEL
[Aside to Prospero] Sir, all this service
Have I done since I went.

PROSPERO
[Aside to Ariel] My tricksy spirit!

ALONSO
These are not natural events; they strengthen
From strange to stranger—Say, how came you hither?

BOATSWAIN
If I did think, sir, I were well awake,
I'd strive to tell you. We were dead of sleep,
And,—how, we know not,—all clapp'd under hatches,
Where, but even now, with strange and several noises
Of roaring, shrieking, howling, jingling chains,
And mo diversity of sounds, all horrible,
We were awak'd; straightway, at liberty:
Where we, in all her trim, freshly beheld
Our royal, good, and gallant ship; our master
Cap'ring to eye her: on a trice, so please you,
Even in a dream, were we divided from them,
And were brought moping hither.

ARIEL
[Aside to Prospero] Was't well done?

PROSPERO
[Aside to Ariel] Bravely, my diligence. Thou shalt be free.

ALONSO
This is as strange a maze as e'er men trod;
And there is in this business more than nature

Was ever conduct of: some oracle
Must rectify our knowledge.

PROSPERO
Sir, my liege,
Do not infest your mind with beating on
The strangeness of this business: at pick'd leisure,
Which shall be shortly, single I'll resolve you,—
Which to you shall seem probable—of every
These happen'd accidents; till when, be cheerful
And think of each thing well.—*[Aside to Ariel]* Come hither, spirit;
Set Caliban and his companions free;
Untie the spell. *[Exit Ariel]* How fares my gracious sir?
There are yet missing of your company
Some few odd lads that you remember not.

*[Re-enter Ariel, driving in Caliban, Stephano, and Trinculo,
in their stolen apparel.]*

STEPHANO
Every man shift for all the rest, and let no man take care for himself, for all is but fortune.—Coragio! bully-monster, Coragio!

TRINCULO
If these be true spies which I wear in my head, here's a goodly sight.

CALIBAN
O Setebos, these be brave spirits indeed.
How fine my master is! I am afraid
He will chastise me.

SEBASTIAN
Ha, ha!
What things are these, my lord Antonio?
Will money buy them?

ANTONIO
Very like; one of them
Is a plain fish, and, no doubt, marketable.

PROSPERO
Mark but the badges of these men, my lords,
Then say if they be true.—This mis-shapen knave—
His mother was a witch; and one so strong
That could control the moon, make flows and ebbs,
And deal in her command without her power.
These three have robb'd me; and this demi-devil,—
For he's a bastard one,—had plotted with them
To take my life: two of these fellows you
Must know and own; this thing of darkness I
Acknowledge mine.

CALIBAN
I shall be pinch'd to death.

ALONSO
Is not this Stephano, my drunken butler?

SEBASTIAN
He is drunk now: where had he wine?

ALONSO
And Trinculo is reeling-ripe: where should they
Find this grand liquor that hath gilded them?
How cam'st thou in this pickle?

TRINCULO
I have been in such a pickle since I saw you last that, I fear me,
will never out of my bones. I shall not fear fly-blowing.

SEBASTIAN
Why, how now, Stephano!

STEPHANO
O! touch me not: I am not Stephano, but a cramp.

PROSPERO
You'd be king o' the isle, sirrah?

STEPHANO
I should have been a sore one, then.

ALONSO
This is as strange a thing as e'er I look'd on.

[Pointing to Caliban]

PROSPERO
He is as disproportioned in his manners
As in his shape.—Go, sirrah, to my cell;
Take with you your companions: as you look
To have my pardon, trim it handsomely.

CALIBAN
Ay, that I will; and I'll be wise hereafter,
And seek for grace. What a thrice-double ass
Was I, to take this drunkard for a god,
And worship this dull fool!

PROSPERO
Go to; away!

ALONSO
Hence, and bestow your luggage where you found it.

SEBASTIAN
Or stole it, rather.

[Exeunt Caliban, Stephano, and Trinculo]

PROSPERO
Sir, I invite your Highness and your train
To my poor cell, where you shall take your rest
For this one night; which—part of it—I'll waste
With such discourse as, I not doubt, shall make it
Go quick away; the story of my life
And the particular accidents gone by
Since I came to this isle: and in the morn
I'll bring you to your ship, and so to Naples,
Where I have hope to see the nuptial
Of these our dear-belov'd solemnized;
And thence retire me to my Milan, where
Every third thought shall be my grave.

ALONSO
I long To hear the story of your life, which must
Take the ear strangely.

PROSPERO
I'll deliver all;
And promise you calm seas, auspicious gales,
And sail so expeditious that shall catch
Your royal fleet far off.—*[Aside to Ariel]* My Ariel, chick,
That is thy charge: then to the elements
Be free, and fare thou well!—Please you, draw near.

[Exeunt]

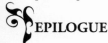

EPILOGUE

[Spoken by Prospero]

Now my charms are all o'erthrown,
And what strength I have's mine own;
Which is most faint; now 'tis true,
I must be here confin'd by you,

Or sent to Naples. Let me not,
Since I have my dukedom got,
And pardon'd the deceiver, dwell
In this bare island by your spell:
But release me from my bands
With the help of your good hands.
Gentle breath of yours my sails
Must fill, or else my project fails,
Which was to please. Now I want
Spirits to enforce, art to enchant;
And my ending is despair,
Unless I be reliev'd by prayer,
Which pierces so that it assaults
Mercy itself, and frees all faults.
As you from crimes would pardon'd be,
Let your indulgence set me free.

END

5245134R0

Made in the USA
Lexington, KY
19 April 2010